THIS BOOK
BELONGS TO:

mantra lingua

_____

_____

_____

For Anna
M.W.

For Sebastian,
David & Candlewick
H.O.

Published by arrangement with Walker Books Ltd, London

Dual language edition first published 2006
by Mantra Lingua
Global House, 303 Ballards Lane, London N12 8NP
http://www.mantralingua.com

Text copyright © 1991 Martin Waddell
Illustrations copyright © 1991 Helen Oxenbury
Dual language copyright © 2006 Mantra Lingua
Kurdish translation by Anwar Soltani

مراوی وەرزێر

FARMER DUCK

written by
Martin Waddell

illustrated by
Helen Oxenbury

mantra lingua

هەبوو نەبوو مراوییەک بوو تووشی نەهامەتی
هاتبوو چونکە لەگەڵ وەرزێرێکی تەمبەلی پیر دەژیا.
مراوییەکە ئیشی دەکرد. وەرزێرەکەش بەدرێژایی
رۆژ لەناو جێگەکەیدا پاڵ دەکەوت.

There once was a duck who had the bad luck
to live with a lazy old farmer.
The duck did the work.
The farmer stayed
all day in bed.

مراوی مانگای لە مەزرا دەهێنایەوە ماڵ.
وەرزێر دەیپرسی: "کاروبار چۆن بەڕێوە دەچن؟"
مراوی وەڵامی دەدایەوە: "کواک!"

The duck fetched the cow from the field.
"How goes the work?"
called the farmer.
The duck answered,
"Quack!"

مراوی مەڕی لەسەر گردەکەوە دەهێنایەوە ماڵ.

وەرزێر دەیپرسی: "کاروبار چۆن بەڕێوە دەچن؟"

مراوی وەڵامی دەدایەوە: "کواک!"

The duck brought the sheep from the hill.
"How goes the work?" called the farmer.
The duck answered,
"Quack!"

مراوی مریشکەکانی دادەکردە ناو کۆلانە.

وەرزێر دەیپرسی: "کاروبار چۆن بەڕێوە دەچن؟"

مراوی وەڵامی دەدایەوە: "کواک!"

The duck put the hens in their house.
"How goes the work?"
called the farmer.
The duck answered,
"Quack!"

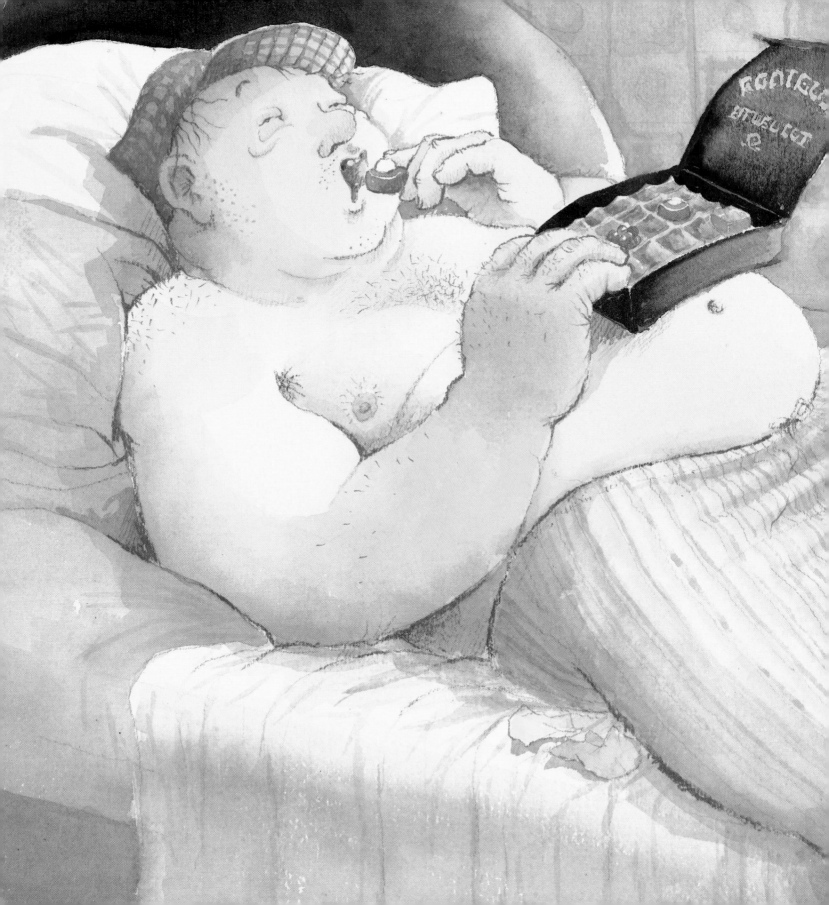

وەرزێر ئەوەندە لە جێگەدا مابوەوە، قەڵەو ببوو و مراوی

بەستەزمانیش لە ئیش و کاری ڕۆژ هەتا ئێوارە تەواو جاڕز ببوو.

The farmer got fat through staying in bed
and the poor duck got fed up
with working all day.

"كاروبار چۆن بەڕێوه دەچن؟"
"کواک!"

"How goes the work?"
"QUACK!"

"کاروبار چۆن بەڕێوه دەچن؟"
"کواک!"

"How goes the work?"
"QUACK!"

"كاروبار چۆن بەڕێوه دەچن؟"
"کواک!"

"How goes the work?"
"QUACK!"

"كاروبار چۆن بەڕێوه دەچن؟"
"کواک!"

"How goes the work?"
"QUACK!"

"کاروبار چۆن بەرێوە دەچن؟"
"کواک!"

"How goes the work?"
"QUACK!"

"کاروبار چۆن بەرێوە دەچن؟"
"کواک!"

"How goes the work?"
"QUACK!"

مراوی بەستەزمان خەواڵۆ
و چاو بەگریان و ماندوو بوو.

The poor duck was sleepy
and weepy
and tired.

مریشک و مانگا و مەڕیش زۆر بەوە دڵتەنگ بوون.
ئەوان مراوییان خۆش دەویست.
هەر بۆیەش لەبەر مانگەشەو کۆڕێکیان بەست
و پلانێکیان بۆ بەیانی رۆژی دواتر دانا.

مانگا گوتی: "مەع!"
مەڕ گوتی: "باع!"
مریشکەکان گوتیان: "جیک جیک!"

پلانەکەش هەر **ئەوە** بوو.

The hens and the cow
and the sheep got very
upset.
They loved the duck.
So they held a meeting
under the moon and
they made a plan
for the morning.

"MOO!" said the cow.
"BAA!" said the sheep.
"CLUCK!" said the hens.
And THAT was the plan!

پێش ئەوەی خۆر هەڵبێت، حەوشی مەزراکە
چۆڵ بوو مانگا و مەڕ و مریشکەکان بەئەسپایی
لە دەرگای پشتەوە چوونە ناوماڵەکە.

It was just before dawn and the farmyard was still.
Through the back door and into the house
crept the cow and the sheep and the hens.

بێدەنگێک گەیشتنە ناو داڵانەکە.
بەجیرەجیر لە پلیکانەکان
سەرکەوتن.

They stole down the hall.
They creaked
up the stairs.

خۆیان لەژێر قەرەوێڵەی وەرزێرەکەدا شاردەوە
و بەربوونە جووڵانەوە و پێکداهاتن.
قەرەوێڵەکە کەوتە تەکان و شەکان،
وەرزێر لە خەو راپەڕی
و گوتی: "کاروبار چۆن بەڕێوە دەچن؟" ئینجا...

They squeezed under the bed of
the farmer and wriggled about.
The bed started to rock and the
farmer woke up, and he called,
"How goes the work?"
and...

"مەع!"
"باع!"
"جیک جیک!"

"MOO!"
"BAA!"
"CLUCK!"

تێکڕا قەرەوێڵەیان بەرز کردەوە و کابرا هاواری لێ هەستا.
وەرزێری پیریان هەڵگرت و بە زەوییاندا کوتا و کوتا،
هەتا لەسەر قەرەوێڵەکە کەوتە خوارەوە...

They lifted his bed and he started to shout, and they banged
and they bounced the old farmer about and about and about,
right out of the bed...

ئینجا وەرزێر هەڵات و مانگا و مەڕ و مریشكیش بەدەوریدا بەربوونه
مەعەمەع و باعەباع و جیكەجیك.

and he fled with the cow and the sheep and the hens
mooing and baaing and clucking around him.

رايكرده ناو كۆڵان...
"مەع!"

Down the lane...
"Moo!"

بەناو مەزرادا...
"باع!"

through the fields...
"Baa!"

بەسەر گردەکەدا...
"جیک جیک!"

over the hill...
"Cluck!"

ئیتر هەرگیز نەگەڕایەوە.

and he never came back.

مراوی لە خەو هەستا،
بە شەکەتی و شەلەشەل
چووە حەوشە.
لەوێ چاوەڕوان بوو گوێی لێ بێت
بڵێن: "کاروبار چۆن بەڕێوە دەچن؟"
بەڵام کەس هیچی نەگوت!

The duck awoke and waddled wearily into the yard expecting
to hear, "How goes the work?"
But nobody spoke!

مانگا و مەڕ و مریشکەکان هاتنەوە.

مراوی گوتی: "کواک؟"

مانگا گوتی: "مەع!"

مەڕ گوتی: "باع!"

مریشکەکان گوتیان: "جیک جیک!"

کە ئەوە هەموو نەقڵەکەی بۆ مراوی گێڕایەوە.

Then the cow and the sheep and the
hens came back.
"Quack?" asked the duck.
"Moo!" said the cow.
"Baa!" said the sheep.
"Cluck!" said the hens.
Which told the duck
the whole story.

ئینجا به مەعەمەع و باعەباع و جیکەجیک
و کواک کواک بۆ ئیش و کار لە مەزرای
خۆیاندا ئامادە بوون.

Then mooing and baaing
and clucking and quacking
they all set to work
on their farm.

Here are some other bestselling dual language

books from Mantra Lingua

for you to enjoy.